Dear Parent:
Your child's love of re

Every child learns to read in a diff ... speed. Some go back and forth between reading levels and read favorite books again and again. Others read through each level in order. You can help your young reader improve and become more confident by encouraging his or her own interests and abilities. From books your child reads with you to the first books he or she reads alone, there are I Can Read Books for every stage of reading:

SHARED READING
Basic language, word repetition, and whimsical illustrations, ideal for sharing with your emergent reader

BEGINNING READING
Short sentences, familiar words, and simple concepts for children eager to read on their own

READING WITH HELP
Engaging stories, longer sentences, and language play for developing readers

READING ALONE
Complex plots, challenging vocabulary, and high-interest topics for the independent reader

ADVANCED READING
Short paragraphs, chapters, and exciting themes for the perfect bridge to chapter books

I Can Read Books have introduced children to the joy of reading since 1957. Featuring award-winning authors and illustrators and a fabulous cast of beloved characters, I Can Read Books set the standard for beginning readers.

A lifetime of discovery begins with the magical words "I Can Read!"

Visit www.icanread.com for information
on enriching your child's reading experience.

Marley & Me

Marley to the Rescue!

Adapted by M. K. Gaudet

Based on the screenplay written by Scott Frank and Don Roos

Based on the book *Marley & Me: Life and Love with the World's Worst Dog*
by John Grogan published by William Morrow,
an imprint of HarperCollins Publishers in 2005.

HarperCollins®, 🐾®, and I Can Read Book® are trademarks of HarperCollins Publishers.

Library of Congress catalog card number: 2008933159
ISBN 978-0-06-170437-6

❖

First Edition

I Can Read!

BEGINNING 1 READING

Marley & Me

Marley to the Rescue!

HarperCollins*Publishers*

This is Marley.

He is a very friendly and silly dog.

Marley has lots of fun when he breaks things and makes big messes. Look at Marley play with his toy on the sofa!

John and Jenny are Marley's owners.

They got Marley when he was

just a little puppy.

They love him

even when he is bad.

Marley is a member of the family.

Marley really likes the
newest member of the family.
His name is Patrick.

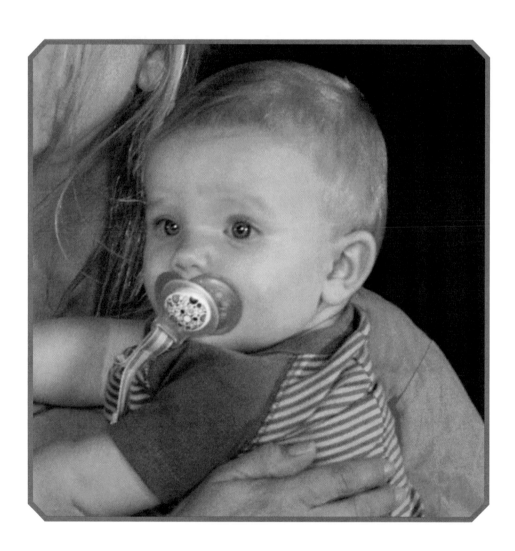

Marley and his family

live in a yellow house.

Marley likes the girl who lives next door. Her name is Lisa. Marley likes to chew on her sneakers!

One day, Marley hears something
that makes him growl
at the window.
A girl outside yells for help.

Everyone dashes outside.

It's getting dark.

"Call the police," says John.

Jenny is worried.

John and Marley find

the girl in trouble

close to their house.

It is Lisa!

A bad man grabbed her

and stole her purse.

She was very scared.

John sits down with Lisa for a while
and makes her feel better.
"It's okay. I've got you," says John.

John is so upset Lisa was hurt,

he does not notice

when he drops Marley's leash.

Oh, no!

The dog is gone!

Where can he be?

"Marley! Marley?" yells John.

WHOOP! WHOOP!
Soon, the police come
to help Lisa.

Who is in the backseat
of the police car?
It is Marley!

"That is our dog!

We are sorry

if he got in your way," says John.

John and Jenny think Marley

has been bad again.

"We would not have found

the thief without him!"

says the policeman.

"This dog followed the smell

of the robber to the gas station.

He kept the man cornered

until we arrived!"

"What a good dog!" says John.

"Yes, he is!" says the officer.

"Woof!" agrees Marley.

Hooray, Marley!

You saved the day!